The Witch Song

Who were the witches? Where did they come from?
Maybe your great, great, great grandma was one.
Witches were wise, wise women they say,
And there's a little witch in every woman today.

Bonnie Lockhart

The Kitchen Witch Promise
To obey the laws of Mother Nature,
to respect and preserve her Queendom
and her works.

PUFFIN CANADA

Published by the Penguin Group

Penguin Group (Canada), 90 Eglinton Avenue East, Suite 700, Toronto, Ontario, Canada M4P 2Y3
(a division of Pearson Canada Inc.)

Penguin Group (USA) Inc., 375 Hudson Street, New York, New York 10014, U.S.A.
Penguin Books Ltd, 80 Strand, London WC2R 0RL, England
Penguin Ireland, 25 St Stephen's Green, Dublin 2, Ireland (a division of Penguin Books Ltd)
Penguin Group (Australia), 250 Camberwell Road, Camberwell, Victoria 3124, Australia (a division of Pearson Australia Group Pty Ltd)
Penguin Books India Pvt Ltd, 11 Community Centre, Panchsheel Park, New Delhi – 110 017, India
Penguin Group (NZ), cnr Airborne and Rosedale Roads, Albany, Auckland 1310, New Zealand (a division of Pearson New Zealand Ltd)
Penguin Books (South Africa) (Pty) Ltd, 24 Sturdee Avenue, Rosebank, Johannesburg 2196, South Africa

Penguin Books Ltd, Registered Offices: 80 Strand, London WC2R 0RL, England

First published 2006

1 2 3 4 5 6 7 8 9 10 (RRD)

Text and illustrations copyright © Blair Drawson, 2006

Manufactured in Mexico.

Library and Archives Canada Cataloguing in Publication data available upon request

Visit the Penguin Group (Canada) website at **www.penguin.ca**

Special and corporate bulk purchase rates available; please see **www.penguin.ca/corporatesales**
or
call 1-800-399-6858, ext. 477 or 474

Witches in the Kitchen

A Year in
the Life of a
Junior Witch

Blair and
Anne Marie
Drawson

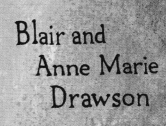

PUFFIN
CANADA

Jan. 1

Dear Grimoire, *

Today is New Year's Day, and I am writing in you for the very first time. In you, Grimoire, I will keep every witch idea that enters my mind. And may no one even so much as dare to pry into my secrets, unless of course they have achieved the rank of Junior Witch!

All violators of this rule can expect to have the Hex Major cast upon them, instantly!

I mean it!

Special note to Aunt Nettle, Aunt Thistle, and Granny Grackle: Please respect my privacy, okay?

Thank you, Ivy
(Jr. Witch)

HERE I AM, POSING BY A
WITCHWOOD TREE IN WINTER.
THE WITCHWOOD — OR ROWAN
OR MOUNTAIN ASH
(TAKE YOUR PICK) —
IS A TREE MOST SACRED
TO WITCHES.

*A GRIMOIRE
OR WITCH'S JOURNAL
OR BOOK OF SHADOWS ARE
ALL PRETTY MUCH THE
SAME THING.

Grimoire,
I might as well confess:
a heartless teacher gave me
an F (for Flunkage) in
Cooking Skills.

Well, so what if my Tuna Noodle Casserole was less than perfect?! (Okay, it was an icky stinkbomb, actually, and the less said about it, the better.) Anyway, the result is that my mother has sent me away for a whole year to learn The Art of Kitchen Witchery from my two spinster* aunts, Thistle and Nettle—oh, and Granny Grackle, too.

Granny Grackle is the senior member of our coven. She is also a Certified Crone, the highest rank in witchcraft, and therefore v-e-r-y respected. You don't get to be a Crone until you have lived for a very long time and learned all sorts of Advanced Witch Lore. Also, your nose and chin must have grown close enough together for you to hold a walnut between them. Granny Grackle passes the Walnut Test with flying colours. Plus, her nose and chin are adorned with several warts, of which she is very proud.

As for my Aunties, they are both Intermediate Witches. That means they are halfway to being full-fledged Crones. Aunt Nettle has the nose (a magnificent one), and Aunt Thistle the chin (equally grand), so I suppose the two of them combined would make up one complete Crone.

Grimoire, my own nose hasn't even started to beak! Ditto for my chin—not a single wart! The Aunties keep telling me my nose is positively cute! Well, I don't want it cute, thank you very much. A cute nose is often unfairly associated with lack of lore.

*SPINSTER
AN UNMARRIED WOMAN. SOME THINK THIS IS A NEGATIVE WORD, BUT WITCHES KNOW IT SIMPLY MEANS A WOMAN WHO SPINS (AS IN WOOL).

My Aunties are true Kitchen Witches. They really know their way
around a cauldron, and they have a pantry full of very witchy things:
a baldness reversal charm from China; an opossum's jawbone
from Appalachia that's supposed to help nursing mothers;
an amulet from a real Egyptian mummy used for fixing any food
that's gotten too salty; resin of dragon's blood
from Peru, used for the double-quick
healing of wounds; and some poisoned arrows
from Africa and a real stuffed Egyptian
cobra (both of which I must be very
careful around). Plus they have a shrunken
head named El Capitán from the Amazon jungle!

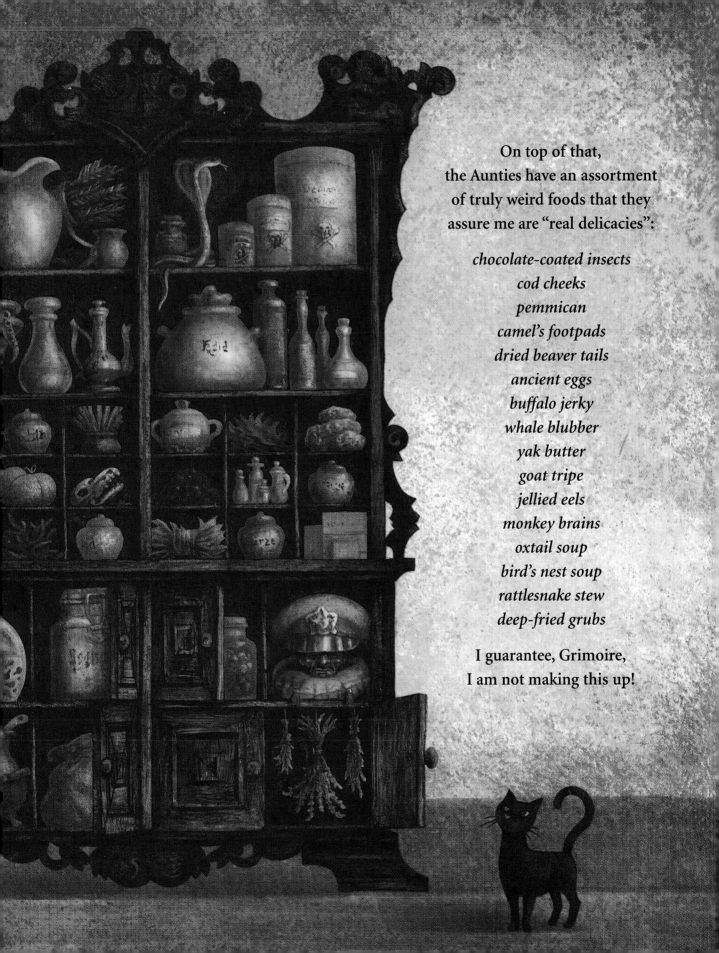

On top of that,
the Aunties have an assortment
of truly weird foods that they
assure me are "real delicacies":

chocolate-coated insects
cod cheeks
pemmican
camel's footpads
dried beaver tails
ancient eggs
buffalo jerky
whale blubber
yak butter
goat tripe
jellied eels
monkey brains
oxtail soup
bird's nest soup
rattlesnake stew
deep-fried grubs

I guarantee, Grimoire,
I am not making this up!

More Lore, Grimoire?
Did you know that...?

Even though the Aunties' delicacies are actual foods, a lot of what witches do in the kitchen (or elsewhere, for that matter) is shrouded in a cloak of secrecy.

Witches use codes, signs, invisible inks, and all sorts of other devices to confuse the non-witch and send the unwary on a wild goose chase. It's all part of the need to shield ourselves from prying eyes and misunderstanding.

You see, in the bad old days, witches were feared. Because of that, they were often deprived of their property and sometimes drowned or burned at the stake even though they didn't do anything wrong! An elderly lady, living alone, perhaps with only a cat to keep her company, was likely to have the darkest suspicions cast upon her and might have been treated in the cruelest way.

Is it any wonder that witches became secretive? Only now are modern witches able and willing to share more of their craft with the outside world.

Everybody has heard of "eye of newt and toe of frog," right?
Also, "wool of bat and tongue of dog"? Those words are from an
old witches' incantation found in Shakespeare's *Macbeth.*
They sound pretty creepy. I mean, who would want to use such nasty,
gruesome ingredients, and for what purpose?

Well, guess what? They weren't really nasty ingredients at all.
It was just witches' code for plants and herbs that could easily be found in
the garden or fields nearby. The code was to prevent people who lacked
lore from making a mess of things—for instance, from trying to
prepare a potion that was beyond their ability. So, "eye of newt" meant
nothing more than a day lily. Or a daisy or black-eyed susan or any flower
that had an "eye." And "tongue of dog" meant "hound's tongue," a common
herb that was said to quiet the barking of dogs. Here are some others:

Candlewick Plant = Mullein
Dwale = Deadly Nightshade
Enchanter's Plant = Vervain
Dew of the Sea = Rosemary
Password = Primrose
Joy of the Mountain = Marjoram
Little Dragon = Tarragon
Seven Years' Love = Yarrow
Sorcerer's Violet = Periwinkle
Bat's Wings = Holly
Calf's Snout = Snapdragon
Love-in-Idleness = Pansy
Loveroot = Orris
Witches' Fingers = Foxglove

Mullein, yarrow, and vervain are three very important herbs
in a witch's pantry and garden. In olden times,
mullein leaves were dried and rolled, and burned
as candlewicks. When powdered, the plant was
known as Graveyard Dust.

Me and
Omen,
shrouded in a
cloak of secrecy

Aunt Nettle decided to do some baking today. The trouble was,

she couldn't quite remember the recipe for Cheeky Chocowitch Cookies. (Grimoire, just between you and me, I have noticed that Granny and my Aunties can be rather forgetful.)

Anyway, I was reading *The Kitchen Witch's Guide to Household Management* when I heard Aunt Nettle call out, "Thistle, dear, do you remember how to make Cheeky Chocowitch Cookies?"

"Negative," came Aunt Thistle's voice from the scullery. "But I thought I saw Omen playing with the recipe book not long ago. Did you ask him?"

I was miffed that no one thought to ask me. Not that it would've done much good, I suppose, since I didn't know either. But I'd have appreciated the gesture. And it would've been easier than trying to get a word out of Omen. Because, you see, he is our familiar.*

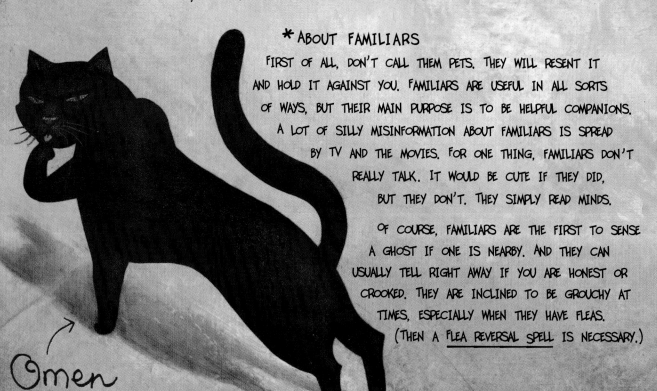

* ABOUT FAMILIARS

FIRST OF ALL, DON'T CALL THEM PETS. THEY WILL RESENT IT AND HOLD IT AGAINST YOU. FAMILIARS ARE USEFUL IN ALL SORTS OF WAYS, BUT THEIR MAIN PURPOSE IS TO BE HELPFUL COMPANIONS. A LOT OF SILLY MISINFORMATION ABOUT FAMILIARS IS SPREAD BY TV AND THE MOVIES. FOR ONE THING, FAMILIARS DON'T REALLY TALK. IT WOULD BE CUTE IF THEY DID, BUT THEY DON'T. THEY SIMPLY READ MINDS.

OF COURSE, FAMILIARS ARE THE FIRST TO SENSE A GHOST IF ONE IS NEARBY. AND THEY CAN USUALLY TELL RIGHT AWAY IF YOU ARE HONEST OR CROOKED. THEY ARE INCLINED TO BE GROUCHY AT TIMES, ESPECIALLY WHEN THEY HAVE FLEAS. (THEN A FLEA REVERSAL SPELL IS NECESSARY.)

Omen

(Grimoire, my Aunties have the greatest, loveliest, smartest, most adorable familiar you could wish for: Omen the Cat! He's like the smart assistant in stories who seems to be invisible but really runs everything. Whenever something truly weird and mysterious happens, you can bet you'll find Omen somewhere nearby, calmly licking a paw and smiling wickedly to himself—as if he were in on some really awesome secret, which he probably is!)

Again Aunt Thistle's voice came booming from the scullery. "Did you think to consult the cauldron, sister?" She emerged, wiping her hands on her apron. "We can always try that."

"Why, yes! Of course," said Aunt Nettle with much enthusiasm.

"Ivy, dear," she turned to me. "Will you put on the kettle, please? We'll all have a nice cup of catnip tea while we prepare the cauldron."

This is me, feeling miffed!

Finbar →

GRANNY GRACKLE HAS A BLACKBIRD FAMILIAR NAMED FINBAR, WHO GOES EVERYWHERE WITH HER, OFTEN RIDING UNDER HER HAT WITH ONLY HIS BEAK PROTRUDING. FINBAR, UNLIKE GRANNY, HAS A TERRIFIC MEMORY, WITH ALMOST 3,000 RECIPES IN HIS HEAD. HE COMMUNICATES WITH HER IN A LANGUAGE ONLY SHE CAN UNDERSTAND. AND HE INDICATES QUANTITIES BY TAPPING HIS BEAK.

So while I made the tea, the Aunties heated up the cauldron and got it good and boiling. Aunt Nettle poured a handful of dried alphabet soup and cast it into the mix. Then while Aunt Thistle stirred the pot, being careful to always move the spoon in a clockwise direction, Aunt Nettle recited the following incantation:

Cauldron, cauldron, now or then,
Who, How, Why? Where or When?
Answer me my question so
I need not ask again.

Then she paused for a moment and asked, "Cauldron, this is a Where question. Where is my recipe for Cheeky Chocowitch Cookies?"

While we waited quietly for the cauldron to gather its thoughts, Aunt Nettle stared into space with a goofy, unfocussed look in her eyes. I realized that she was contributing to the incantation in her own witchy way, by bringing her thoughts into harmony with the cauldron's.

Finally, the alphabet soup letters began to float to the surface. First a **B**, then an **E**, followed by an **H** and an **I, N, D**. The word lingered on the surface for a moment, then drifted away. Then came an **O**, an **M**, an **E**, an **N**, and an **S**. And there it was at last, the complete message:

BEHIND OMENS BED.

"Why, that little demon!" exclaimed the Aunties in unison.

Aunt Nettle hurried off to Omen's sleeping nook and returned a moment later, holding a crumpled slip of paper covered in cobwebs.

"Here it is. The recipe. It was just where the cauldron said it was," she declared with satisfaction. "That rascal of an Omen must have been batting it around with his paws, and it ended up in a corner behind his bed."

We all felt very relieved and celebrated with a large pot of piping hot catnip tea. And, of course, Omen wanted his, too.

April 9

Today I helped Aunt Nettle

with some pesky chores around the house.
Fortunately, Grimoire, we had the cauldron to help us in the Who, How, Why, Where,
and When matters, so questions and details got handled as if by magic.

We were just about finished when Auntie invited me to practise an
Advanced Cauldron Incantation. This is where a qualified witch asks the cauldron
to reveal any deeper secret, or further information, that it wishes us to know.
So, carefully, I recited the incantation, which goes like this:

Cauldron, cauldron, cooking pot,
tell me true or tell me not.
Tell me now the most important
message of the lot.

To our surprise, the cauldron wasted no time in presenting the words

SEE GRANY.

(The cauldron often misspells.)

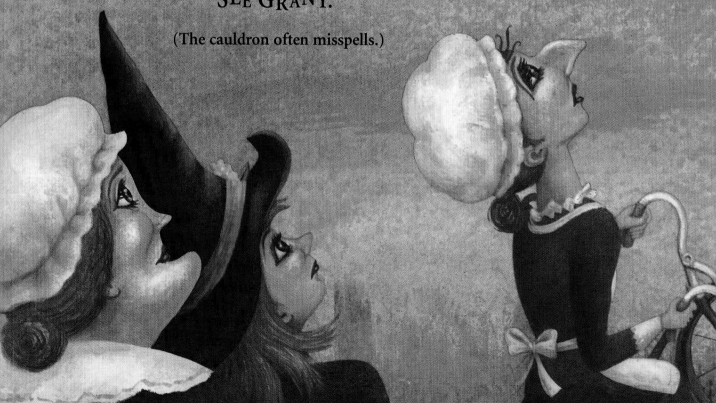

In some alarm, we all hopped on our bikes (well, in my case I rode on Aunt Thistle's
handlebars, since I don't have a bike of my own) and rode to Granny's house,
wondering all the way what on earth could be wrong.

When we arrived at her little cottage, we were treated to the sight of Granny,
in full Crone regalia, riding her broom in swooping loops above the treetops
and cackling with glee.

"Hello, girls!" she shouted merrily. "I see you got my wee message.
Spring is on its way, girls. Spring is on its way!"

"Are you all right, Granny?" we called to her.

"Never better, girls," she called back.
"Never better. Earlier I did feel a wee pain
in my bones, and a spasm in my old toes,
but a spin on the broom cheered me up
very nicely, thank you!"

Broom, Cauldron, and Familiar Lore

NOWADAYS, BROOM FLYING IS CONSIDERED SHOWING OFF, AND IT HAS
FALLEN OUT OF FAVOUR WITH THE MODERN URBAN WITCH.
SHE PREFERS TO GET AROUND BY BICYCLE, BUS, TAXI, OR SUBWAY,
RESERVING THE BROOM FOR SPECIAL OCCASIONS ONLY, SUCH AS
WITCHES' JAMBOREES, AND NEVER BEFORE DARK—THAT'S TOTALLY TABOO!

CRONES, HOWEVER, AND COUNTRY WITCHES IN GENERAL, HAVE A
DIFFERENT ATTITUDE ENTIRELY, AND THEY WILL FLY WHENEVER THE WHIM
STRIKES THEM. GRANNY GRACKLE, OF COURSE, IS ONE OF THESE.
SHE HAS AN ASSORTMENT OF REALLY SPLENDID BROOMS, WHICH
SHE IS ALWAYS TRYING OUT.

FLYING BROOMS ARE CRAFTED BY MALE WITCHES,
LIKE MY DADDY, WHO LIVE DEEP WITHIN FORESTS WHERE
THE BEST WOODS GROW. THE SWEEP PART IS MADE
WITH ROWAN, BIRCH, WILLOW, HAZEL, OR HAWTHORNE TWIGS,
AND IT IS BOUND TO THE BROOM HANDLE, WHICH IS
MADE WITH A HEAVIER STICK OF ASH WOOD, MAPLE,
OR THE BROOM PLANT ITSELF. BY THE WAY, THE TRADITIONAL
NAME FOR A BROOM MADE THIS WAY IS "BESOM" (PRONOUNCED BEEZ'M).

Broom, sweepside up

WITCHES OFTEN STORE THEIR BROOMS BY THE DOORWAY TO THEIR HOMES,
SWEEPSIDE UP, BELIEVING THIS ENSURES THAT UNWELCOME ENERGY
STAYS OUTSIDE. (BUT HERE'S A TIP: YOU CAN ALSO RID YOUR
HOUSE OF DISPLEASING PEOPLE AND NEGATIVE ENERGY BY
SPRINKLING SALT ON THE FLOORS. THEN, AS YOU SWEEP
THE SALT OUT THE DOOR, THE BAD ENERGY GOES FLYING
OUT WITH IT! AND GOOD RIDDANCE, TOO!)

WHEN IT COMES TO CAULDRONS, IT IS NOT UNUSUAL FOR WITCHES TO ACTUALLY TALK TO THEIRS. THEY JUST DO. WITCHES ALSO SPEAK TO THEIR KNIVES AND FORKS AND SPOONS, AS WELL AS TO ANY AND ALL POTS AND PANS. AND ALWAYS WITH PROPER RESPECT! NOT ONLY THAT, BUT WITCHES WILL OFTEN SING OR WHISTLE IN THE KITCHEN, BELIEVING THAT IT GIVES FLAVOUR AND ZEST TO FOOD AND POTIONS, JUST AS MUCH AS HERBS AND SPICES DO.

Cauldron, "thinking"

ALSO, STIRRING THE CAULDRON CLOCKWISE IS STANDARD PROCEDURE IF YOU WANT A SPELL TO SUCCEED OR A RECIPE TO TURN OUT. IT'S ALSO IMPORTANT FOR ALL INCANTATIONS TO BE ACCOMPANIED BY RESPECTFUL SILENCE.

OF COURSE, CAULDRONS APPRECIATE BEING WELL CARED FOR. THIS MEANS KEEPING THEM FRESH AND FREE FROM THE ICKY BUILDUP THAT HAPPENS WHEN CERTAIN POTIONS ARE ALLOWED TO DRY INSIDE (OR SO MY AUNTIES TELL ME).

AS FOR FAMILIARS, THEY COME IN ALL SHAPES AND SIZES. THE COMMONEST ONES ARE CATS, OF COURSE, OR BIRDS, SUCH AS CROWS, HAWKS, OR OWLS. CHICKENS CAN ALSO BE FAMILIARS! OTHER COMMON FAMILIARS ARE BATS, WHICH ARE VERY GOOD FOR THE WITCH WHO LIKES TO STAY UP REALLY LATE, AND GOATS, DEER, BEARS, RATS, OR EVEN INSECTS. DOGS CAN BE FAMILIARS, ESPECIALLY ONES WITH WOLF-LIKE CHARACTERISTICS, LIKE POINTED EARS AND SNOUTS. IN GENERAL, WILD CREATURES MAKE BETTER FAMILIARS—MOST DOGS ARE USUALLY TOO CUDDLY AND DOMESTICATED FOR THAT.

a common Familiar

THE MOST IMPORTANT THING TO KNOW, THOUGH, IS THAT YOUR FAMILIAR MUST ACTUALLY BE EARNED. NO ONE CAN GIVE YOU YOUR FAMILIAR, AND YOU CERTAINLY CAN'T BUY ONE. YOUR FAMILIAR WILL COME TO YOU WHEN YOU ARE READY AND NOT A MOMENT SOONER.

I WONDER WHAT MY FAMILIAR WILL BE?

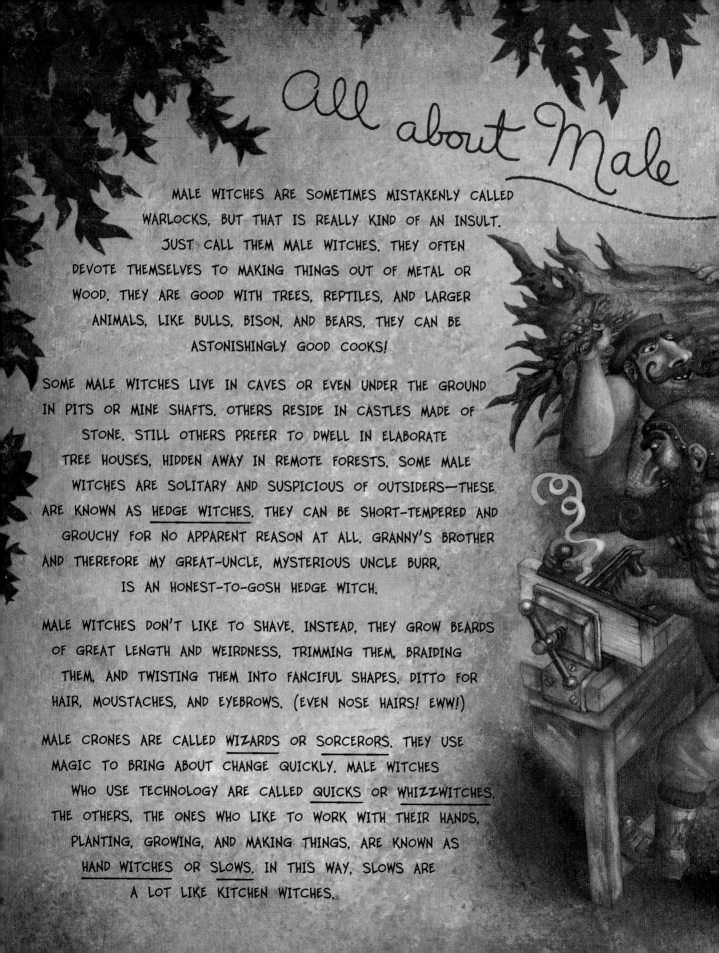

All about Male

MALE WITCHES ARE SOMETIMES MISTAKENLY CALLED
WARLOCKS, BUT THAT IS REALLY KIND OF AN INSULT.
JUST CALL THEM MALE WITCHES. THEY OFTEN
DEVOTE THEMSELVES TO MAKING THINGS OUT OF METAL OR
WOOD. THEY ARE GOOD WITH TREES, REPTILES, AND LARGER
ANIMALS, LIKE BULLS, BISON, AND BEARS. THEY CAN BE
ASTONISHINGLY GOOD COOKS!

SOME MALE WITCHES LIVE IN CAVES OR EVEN UNDER THE GROUND
IN PITS OR MINE SHAFTS. OTHERS RESIDE IN CASTLES MADE OF
STONE. STILL OTHERS PREFER TO DWELL IN ELABORATE
TREE HOUSES, HIDDEN AWAY IN REMOTE FORESTS. SOME MALE
WITCHES ARE SOLITARY AND SUSPICIOUS OF OUTSIDERS—THESE
ARE KNOWN AS HEDGE WITCHES. THEY CAN BE SHORT-TEMPERED AND
GROUCHY FOR NO APPARENT REASON AT ALL. GRANNY'S BROTHER
AND THEREFORE MY GREAT—UNCLE, MYSTERIOUS UNCLE BURR,
IS AN HONEST-TO-GOSH HEDGE WITCH.

MALE WITCHES DON'T LIKE TO SHAVE. INSTEAD, THEY GROW BEARDS
OF GREAT LENGTH AND WEIRDNESS, TRIMMING THEM, BRAIDING
THEM, AND TWISTING THEM INTO FANCIFUL SHAPES. DITTO FOR
HAIR, MOUSTACHES, AND EYEBROWS. (EVEN NOSE HAIRS! EWW!)

MALE CRONES ARE CALLED WIZARDS OR SORCERORS. THEY USE
MAGIC TO BRING ABOUT CHANGE QUICKLY. MALE WITCHES
WHO USE TECHNOLOGY ARE CALLED QUICKS OR WHIZZWITCHES.
THE OTHERS, THE ONES WHO LIKE TO WORK WITH THEIR HANDS,
PLANTING, GROWING, AND MAKING THINGS, ARE KNOWN AS
HAND WITCHES OR SLOWS. IN THIS WAY, SLOWS ARE
A LOT LIKE KITCHEN WITCHES.

Witches

MY DADDY IS A HAND WITCH. HE IS ONE OF
TRIPLETS—THE THREE TREES, AS THEY ARE CALLED.
HIS NAME IS BRAMBLE TREE, AND HIS
TWO BROTHERS ARE BRACKEN AND BRIAR.
(CUTE, YES? WELL, YOU WOULDN'T
THINK SO IF YOU SAW THEM!)

THE THREE TREES ARE FAMOUS FOR
MAKING THE VERY BEST THINGS OUT OF
METAL, AND—YOU GUESSED IT—WOOD!
THEY WORK TOGETHER SO CLOSELY
THAT YOU CAN'T TELL THEM APART,
EXCEPT BY THEIR NOSES AND BEARDS.

THEY MAKE THE BEST CAULDRONS ON
THE PLANET. DITTO FOR THEIR FORKS,
SPOONS, AND HORSESHOES. OUT OF
WOOD THEY MAKE GREAT SIGNS AND
SIGNPOSTS—EITHER CARVED OR MADE TO GROW
THAT WAY, LIKE THE TITLE OF THIS BOOK!
EVERYONE AGREES THAT WHEN IT COMES TO SIGNS,
THE THREE TREES ARE THE BEST. THEIR TRADEMARK
LOOKS LIKE THIS:

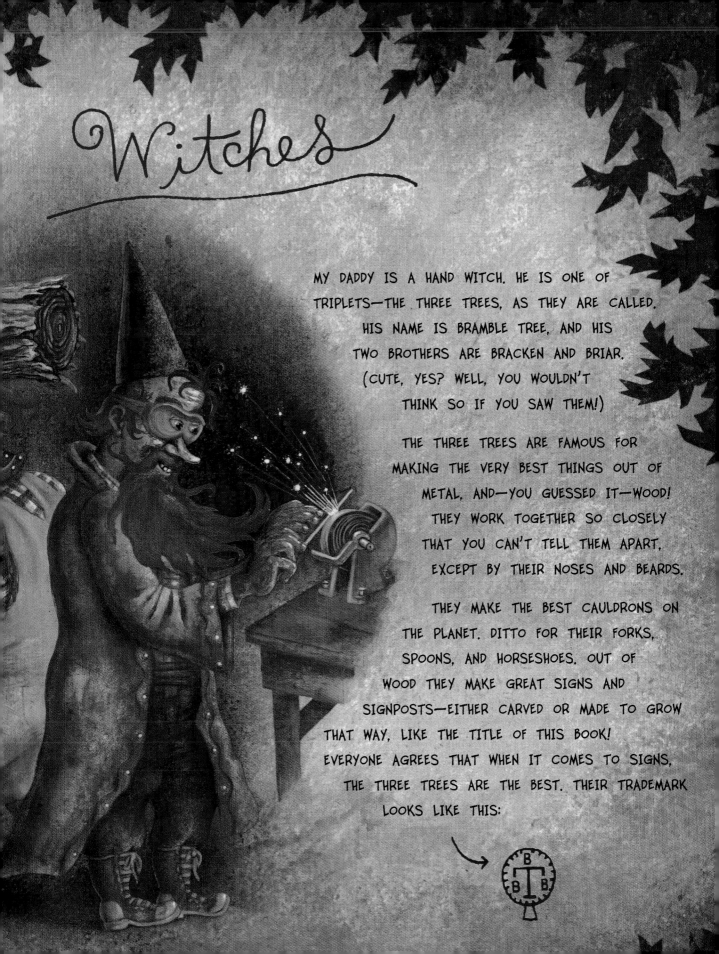

Beltaine—or "May I Make a May Basket?"

Yes, Grimoire, you may. You may gather some goodies—bread, tea,
cookies, cake, honey, fruit, flowers, potpourri—and a poem or a greeting.
Anything nice, especially something you made yourself, with love.
You may decorate your basket with more flowers, leaves, or—*ahem*—ivy!
(That's always nice, right?)

Remember to follow the custom: Leave the May Basket by
the front door of your chosen King or Queen of the May,
then ring the doorbell and run away and hide.
After his or her ecstatic response, you may
come out from hiding, or you may simply
go home, leaving a Mayday Mystery
for your friend to figure out.

Grimoire, the first day of the merry month of May is known to witches as Beltaine—a time of fun and surprises. So today I am going to bring a May Basket to Granny Grackle.

I was just leaving when Aunt Thistle, who has a bunion on her big toe that tells her when the weather is about to change, said to me, "My toe is paining me, Ivy. Better wear a raincoat, dear. It's going to pour."

Well, I don't think so! I mean the weather was absolutely, positively, flawlessly, awesomely BEAUTIFUL. There wasn't so much as one cloud in sight! Sometimes I think my darling Aunties and their silly superstitions are just a little bit old-fashioned. Really.

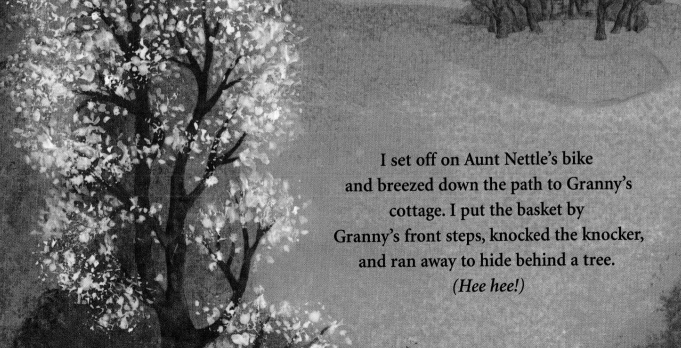

I set off on Aunt Nettle's bike and breezed down the path to Granny's cottage. I put the basket by Granny's front steps, knocked the knocker, and ran away to hide behind a tree. *(Hee hee!)*

When Granny saw the basket, she let out a little
shriek of joy. She knew perfectly well where I was hiding,
of course, but pretended that she didn't.
When she found me, she gave me three things:
  (1) a Granny hug,
  (2) a thank-you for the May Basket, and
  (3) a lecture on how unpredictable the weather can be at Beltaine.

"Now, Ivy, where is your rain cloak, child?" she asked.

"But, Granny," I protested. "Look! It's really warm out.
            There's a beautiful clear blue sky, for gosh sakes."

Granny only shook her head. "No, Ivy, no. It's Beltaine, dear.
A very uncertain time is May Day. Dark clouds are coming,
        and wind and thunderstorms. They'll give you a thrashing.
        Look, lovey, even Finbar says it's so."

At that, Finbar tapped his beak soundly on a block of wood,
            bobbed his head in agreement, and glowered.

Granny was so insistent that I turned the bike around and started
back right away. She gave me a cloak to wear, even though
            the day seemed just as pleasant as ever.

At first I felt hot and sweaty wearing
the cloak, but as I pedalled along,
I noticed a line of creepy dark sky beginning
to form in the west. *Yipes!*
And a stiff wind came up from nowhere.

Oof! The going got tougher … began to struggle
against the wind, while the sky dimmed and grew
dark … felt drops of rain on the brim of my hat …
had to stop and tie my chinstraps
to keep … hat … from blowing … AWAY!

Should have known better than to doubt
a Crone and two Intermediates.

It started to HAIL! There was going
to be—gimmee a break—CHUNKY RAINOLA!

By the time I got home I looked like
something the familiar dragged in. *Drat!*
And a hex upon bad weather surprises!

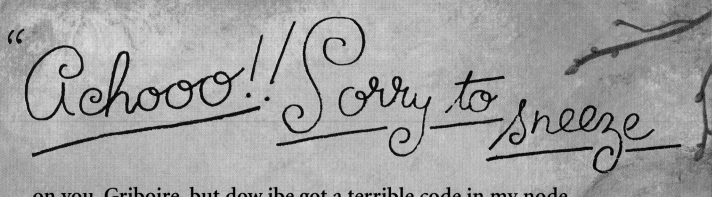

"Achooo!! Sorry to sneeze

on you, Griboire, but dow ibe got a terrible code in my node.

You know the feeling—wheezing and sneezles, aches and chills, teeth chattering,
a nose that should be wearing Nikes ('cause it's running, get it? *hee hee hee*)—
well, when this happens, the Aunties go into Code Red High Alert
Nursing Mode and before long they have trotted out their entire motherlode
of herbal remedies: tinctures, salves, balms, and other evil-smelling
preparations. The thing is, as all Kitchen Witches know, they work! Eventually.

Personally, I prefer to snuggle deep in bed
with a hot bowl of Chickenwitch Soup.
For dessert, a bonbon or three would
be welcome and, for diversion,
some paper dolls.
Or … TWIG PEOPLE!

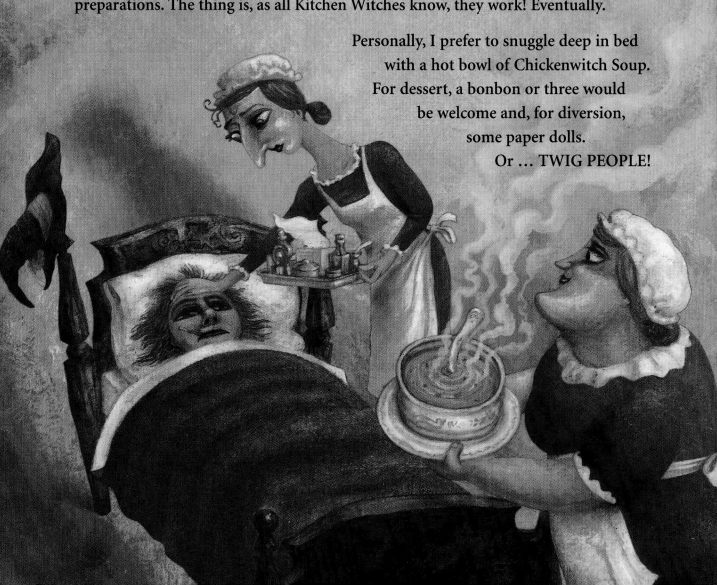

When you find yourself in the woods, or in your own yard with nothing to do, take a few moments to make Twig People. They are made from a variety of natural materials and come in all shapes and sizes.

You can make Twig People from pieces of wood, twigs, bark, leaves, berries, grass, flowers, acorns, pebbles, and whatever else appeals to you. Twig People made from pressed and dried leaves and flowers last longer, but some Twig People aren't meant to survive for very long. It depends on what they are made of—and anything goes!

Ivy's Twig People

You may want to use a bit of glue, string, or paint to put on the finishing touches. You can hang your Twig People from loops of string or grass, or you can simply prop them up on rocks or in tree branches (where they are particularly attractive to the Little Folk).

Twig People make good gifts for friends and relatives. You can even make one using catnip for your feline familiar. Some call them Corn Dollies or Leaf People or Bud Critters, but whatever you call them, they're a lot of fun to make. (Just don't call them Late for Dinner—they hate that! *Hee hee!*)

Yay, hooray! June 21

Midsummer's Day!

Yay, hooray! It's Midsummer's Day!
That means, Grimoire, we're all going to:

(a) have a midnight picnic,
(b) make a great bonfire,
(c) frolic wildly in the woods, and
(d) let our witchy hair down.

The 21st of June is a holiday that is especially important to Kitchen Witches because it's a celebration of Life, Growing Things, and most of all, the Sun.

And guess what, Grimoire? As a special deal, the eve of Midsummer's Day this year will also have a *full moon*. So, with this double-decker extravaganza, witches everywhere will really be having an all-out, rock-your-socks-off jamboree!

(*Ahem.* This is also the day when I—me, yours truly, Ivy—am officially twelve and a half years old. *Yay!*)

Anyway, on the eve of the great day, the Aunties and I went to Granny Grackle's.

Of course, Omen came too, riding with me in a basket on Aunt Thistle's bike. Granny's house is at the edge of an awesome forest. A short skip down a narrow path and there you are, in a clearing in the deep woods—a perfect setting for celebrating Nature.

As we walked along, Aunt Nettle pointed out the plants that are especially important on Midsummer's Day.

"You see, Ivy," she said, "all things yellow are said to reinforce the strength of the sun. So dandelions, buttercups, and black-eyed susans would be good to weave into our hair as garlands. And daisies, too, because of their bright yellow centres."

"Oh yes, Ivy. And oak leaves and climbing greens—*tee hee*—like ivy itself," Granny Grackle cackled.

The deep green leaves reflect the abundance of the Green Man, she said. He represents the growing energy of plant life. Sometimes you can see his green face in treetops or in clusters of leaves. It's like one minute he's *there*, and the next minute, *not*. He can seem a little spooky, but it's really a good sign when he appears.

"And we mustn't forget the Little People," warned Aunt Thistle. "The Fairies, Ivy—the Brownies and the Wood Sprites—Midsummer's Day is a festival for them, too."

By now it was beginning to get dark, so we all got busy. The Aunties laid out the picnic spread. I gathered dry wood for the fire. Omen prowled through the forest, looking for who-knows-what. And Finbar perched on a nearby bush.

The Moon came up looking like a
big fat orange. As the Senior Witch,
it was Granny's privilege to light the
bonfire. She took out a wooden match,
struck it on a nearby rock, and set
the dry moss, twigs, and larger pieces
of wood ablaze. *Yay!* We had a bonfire!

We wove leaves and yellow flowers together
to make garlands, which we placed on one
another's heads. We took out our musical
instruments and began to play.
Aunt Nettle banged on a drum,
Aunt Thistle strummed the ukulele,
and I tootled on my recorder. Granny
had left her bagpipes at home, since
that's an instrument to be played
solo or with other pipers.

Keeping an eye on the fire,
we had a great yummy feast.
The celebration of Midsummer calls for
   any natural food that has already ripened.
We had home-baked bread and yellow cheese
   with watercress, fresh field greens, and
wild strawberries. And we all drank
   Pink-and-Foamy Fairy Punch.

When fireflies appeared, Aunt Thistle
mistook them for a flight of Fairies
   and talked to them, for gosh sakes!
And what fun when we danced!
   Granny and the Aunties let down their
hair (which is really long and witchy),
   and it flew in swirls and tangles.
But did we care? No, we did not!

Standing under an Elderbush at Midsummer will help you see the Little People

At last the stars dimmed and the first light of dawn began to glow. The great moment arrived. A tiny pinprick of brilliant light appeared on the eastern horizon. The first blaze of the purest energy—the Sun!

We all held hands facing the ball of light and said, "O Father Sun, we greet thee and give thanks for your great warmth, your loving light, and your ability to make living things increase. Without you, the Earth would be no more than a dead, icy darkness. We thank you for the life you provide and support."

MIDSUMMER IS WHEN THE SUN CLIMBS TO ITS HIGHEST POINT NORTH OF THE EQUATOR. IT'S ALSO THE LONGEST DAY AND THE SHORTEST NIGHT OF THE YEAR. FATHER SUN IS AT HIS GREATEST STRENGTH, BUT IT'S HIS LIMIT TOO, AND AFTER THIS DAY HE WEAKENS AND BEGINS TO RETURN SOUTH AGAIN. HE PASSES OVER THE EQUATOR DURING THE AUTUMNAL EQUINOX IN SEPTEMBER. HE CONTINUES HIS JOURNEY AND REACHES THE MAXIMUM DISTANCE FROM US DURING THE WINTER SOLSTICE. THAT'S THE OPPOSITE OF MIDSUMMER AND HAS THE SHORTEST DAY OF THE YEAR AND THE LONGEST NIGHT, BECAUSE IT MEANS THAT THE SUN IS READY TO TURN AROUND AND COME BACK TO THOSE OF US WHO LIVE NORTH OF THE EQUATOR. IT'S ANOTHER TIME OF CELEBRATION. WITCHES KNOW THAT DAY, DECEMBER 21, AS "YULE"—PSST! IT'S ALSO MY BIRTHDAY!

The Family Tree of...

Ivy Prickle Tree!! ♀

The Aunties

The Tree Bros.

Nettle ♀   Thistle ♀   Thorn Prickle ♂   Bracken ♂

Bramble Tree ♂   Briar ♂

The Prickle Clan

The Tree Clan

The mysterious Uncle

Clan

Angus ♂   Fergus ♂   Fiona ♀   Granny Grackle Grackle McCracken ♀   Burr ♂   Magnus ♂ Prickle   Cousin   Delilah Rose ♀

Other branches of the Tree clan

The McCracken Clan

The Hawkins Clan

Mary 'Meg' Hawkins ♀   Joe ♂ Tree

Oct. 31

It's Samhain!

or *Halloween,* as some call it,
Grimoire—a time when every witch is buzzing
with excitement, tuning up her broom, forming
covens, telling jokes, and generally getting ready
for the biggest witchfest of the year. Oh, the parties,
Grimoire! The bonfires, the music and dancing,
the cavorting, the, the—I don't know what!

The Aunties spent all day making
Newt Noodles, Giant's Eyeballs,
Sugar Fangs, and other assorted
trick-or-treat sweets for the little kids
who would soon be coming to the door.
Then the Aunties would be off
to join the festivities.

Anyway, in the midst of our preparations, Aunt Nettle was horrified to discover we were imminently in danger of running out of honey. That just wouldn't do, as Giant's Eyeballs without sufficient sticky stuff oozing out of them simply aren't the real thing.

"Hold the fort 'til I get back, sister," she hollered, hopping on her bike and pedalling away to the beekeeper's.

"No problem," Aunt Thistle replied. She was busy carving a jack-o'-lantern for the window. She stepped back to admire her creation and then decided it just wasn't quite finished. "It needs something," she observed. "Doesn't it, Ivy?"

Then it came to her. "Wouldn't it be neat if Jack were wearing sunglasses?" She rummaged around and found an old pair of Granny's that hadn't been worn in many years. Soon Jack was looking very, very cool in his shades.

She lit the candle.

Now, what Aunt Thistle didn't realize was that those sunglasses were so old that the material they were made of (ancient plastic) was highly flammable! When she went to carry the jack-o'-lantern to the window, the sunglasses BURST into HUMUNGOUS FLAMES!

"Eeeeeeeeeeeeeeeee-eeeeeek!"

she shrieked, running around the room in circles, fire fanning out all around her head.

What do you do with a grinning, flaming pumpkin face when you're holding it right in your HANDS, for gosh sakes? Omen, who is normally good in emergencies, took one look and hightailed it out the nearest open window.

Just then, Aunt Nettle pulled up on
her bicycle. Seeing great dancing flames
through the window, she threw down the bike
and ran in. "The think, Sissle, the think!"
she spluttered. "I mean—the sink, Thistle, the sink!"

Aunt Thistle got the message. She raced to the sink
and dumped the jack-o'-lantern in. Quickly,
she turned on the water. Stinky black smoke
shot up into the air with a hiss.

IN THE ANCIENT CELTIC LANGUAGE
SAMHAIN MEANT "THE END OF SUMMER." AND JUST AS WE
MISS THE WARM DAYS OF SUMMER, WE ALSO MISS
OUR DEAD ANCESTORS AT SAMHAIN. FOR THAT REASON,
IT HAS ALWAYS BEEN ASSOCIATED WITH
GHOSTS AND SKELETONS. SOME WITCHES ALSO
CELEBRATE IT AS A SORT OF NEW YEAR, SO
IT'S BOTH A HALLOWED EVE (AS IN HALLOWE'EN)
AND A TIME FOR WITCHY PARTIES.

THE FIRST JACK-O'-LANTERNS WERE CARVED FROM
LARGE TURNIPS OR BEETS AND OFTEN CARRIED
A BURNING COAL INSIDE. HOLES WERE CARVED
TO LET OUT THE LIGHT. PUMPKINS WERE
MOSTLY UNKNOWN IN EUROPE AT THE TIME.
THE PUMPKIN JACK-O'-LANTERN THAT WE ALL
KNOW AND LOVE IS AN AMERICAN INVENTION.

What a mess! After that,
the jack-o'-lantern's
expression seemed
kind of wonky and glum,
but the panic was over.

The Aunties made a nice pot of tea to soothe their jangled nerves.
Soon feeling better, they donned their Samhain costumes and took off,
pausing only to wave goodbye and call out,
"*Ta-ta*, Ivy. Don't wait up for us!"

And that left me to
deal with the ghosts,
the goblins, and the
very scary witches.

Ivy's Do's and Don'ts !!

Even witches have rules. Here are some:

Witches **do** protect the environment.
We clean up our messes and those of our familiars.
(Yuck.) We ride non-polluting vehicles whenever
possible—our brooms!

Witches **do** wear aprons.
Kitchen Witches take pride in our appearance and
dislike flour or spatters of batter on our lovely
black garments. As the saying goes, "Witches wear any
colour, as long as it's black." (Well, *sometimes* white.)

Witches **do** have gardens.
Witches are the original nature girls. Country
witches grow their own veggies. Even big-city witches
have window boxes for growing their own fresh
herbs, flowers, and vegetables. And witches do eat all
of their veggies—even their cauliflower and lima beans.

Witches **do** prefer low tech.
That means candles over electric lights, bicycles and
horses over cars, and handwritten letters over email
(which some Kitchen Witches call "eek-mail").

Witches **do** prefer the Moon over the Sun.
Many witches have sensitive skin and a great number
of them are redheads, who are easily sunburned
(such as, *ahem*, yours truly!). Whenever you see a sunburnt
redheaded person, you *may* be looking at a witch *incognito*.

Witches **don't** argue while cooking food.
Food prepared in an "angry cauldron" can lead to
indigestion and, *ahem*, gas.

Witches **don't** complain about the weather.
Senior Witches can, however, change it when
necessary, through their advanced craft.

Witches **don't** waste.
All kitchen scraps go into the compost pile.
Also, we don't leave the lights on or candles burning
when there is no one in the room.

Witches **don't** prepare potions under a waning moon.
They won't turn out.

Witches **don't** forget their manners.
Nor do they diss people unnecessarily. Witches are
actually quite considerate of others, and any behaviour
to the contrary is thought to be very unwitchlike.

Witches **don't** use the Hex Major.
Well, they **do**, but very sparingly. So unless you have
deeply hurt some witch's feelings, you won't likely be
transformed into some lower form of life (toad, eel,
hedgehog, etc.). The Hex Minor, however, is used much
more often. It is most likely to be used against people
who are rude, gossipy, or inconsiderate. Such people
may find themselves absolutely unable to speak for a
considerable time. Or they may break out in an
unbearable itch. Or they may become totally absent-
minded—sometimes even forgetting the names of their
closest friends!

Witches **don't** eat children.
At least vegetarian witches don't.
(Hee hee!)

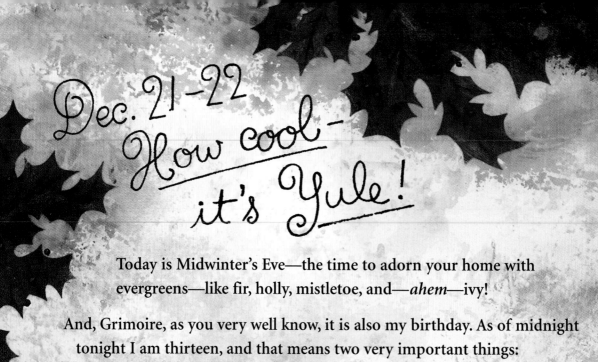

Dec. 21-22
How cool—
it's Yule!

Today is Midwinter's Eve—the time to adorn your home with evergreens—like fir, holly, mistletoe, and—*ahem*—ivy!

And, Grimoire, as you very well know, it is also my birthday. As of midnight tonight I am thirteen, and that means two very important things:

(1) I am a teenager … *and* …

(2) I am now officially an Intermediate Witch (Junior Grade). *Yippee, Yahoo, and Yay!*

Many witches from covens near and far will be gathering tonight at Granny Grackle's cottage for a madcap, magical Yule Costume Party. The theme for this year is "Come as Your Own Familiar," so the Aunties and I will be all decked out as Omen the Cat. What a hoot!

The Aunties invited The Three Trees, Cousin Delilah Rose (from Louisiana), Mysterious Uncle Burr (the Hedge Witch), Baba Yaga (from Russia), La Strega (from Italy), Señorita Consuela, La Curandera (from Panama), and my own magical Mom, Thorn Prickle Tree! How's that for a lineup, Grimoire?

Granny is using an Expansion Spell to convert a small broom closet in her little house to a very grand ballroom. That way everyone can display their costumes in full glory, without any toes, paws, or claws getting stepped on. I can't wait! *Hee hee!*

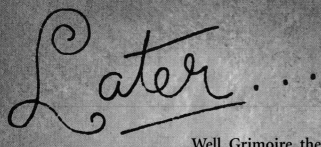

Later...

Well, Grimoire, the party couldn't have been better if it tried! Everyone had a great time, especially me.

The Winter Solstice is the longest night of the year, and this year there was no Moon at all, so it was a dark night, too. This relaxed Mysterious Uncle Burr, who suffers from a strange Moon Affliction. He totally danced the night away with Cousin Delilah Rose. It was funny to see a hedgehog dancing with an owl. My uncles, The Three Trees, were charming as usual, and Mom and Dad looked like they were made for each other.

But here's what I've been dying to tell you, Grimoire! This is what I got for my birthday (along with a whole load of other awesomely neat things):

First—*a new book* from Aunts Nettle and Thistle. They specially bound it and charged it with energy, so it is all ready to receive Kitchen Witch ideas as my next Grimoire. And—get this—it won't even be visible to the non-witch!

Next—*a black feather* from the bosom of Finbar. This was selected and charmed by Granny for use as a wand. Right now, it is only for setting spells—to make sure they don't dissolve before their time. As my skills improve, its power will grow with me. Cool, huh?

And last of all—*my very own broom!* The Three Trees all had a hand in making it, with Daddy Bramble putting on the finishing touches. Then Mom enchanted it with the power to fly true, so that it may not wander off course but must always deliver me to my chosen destination. "Like an arrow," Mom said. "Straight to its target." And it *shall* come when called for.

Its name is Beaudelaire.

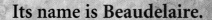

Goodbye then, Grimoire.
This is just about your last page. It's been fun and a great year! Now I'm looking forward to the next one. Thanks for being my book of lore and witchery.
Love, Ivy ♡